FOCUS ON ARTIFICIAL INTELLIGENCE

THE DANGERS OF ARTIFICIAL INTELLIGENCE

by Jennifer Kaul

BrightPoint Press

San Diego, CA

© 2025 BrightPoint Press
an imprint of ReferencePoint Press, Inc.
Printed in the United States

For more information, contact:
BrightPoint Press
PO Box 27779
San Diego, CA 92198
www.BrightPointPress.com

ALL RIGHTS RESERVED.

No part of this work covered by the copyright hereon may be reproduced or used in any form or by any means—graphic, electronic, or mechanical, including photocopying, recording, taping, web distribution, or information storage retrieval systems—without the written permission of the publisher.

LIBRARY OF CONGRESS CATALOGING-IN-PUBLICATION DATA

Name: Kaul, Jennifer, author.
Title: The Dangers of Artificial Intelligence / by Jennifer Kaul.
Description: San Diego, CA: BrightPoint Press, Inc., 2025 | Series: Focus on Artificial
  Intelligence | Audience: Grade 7 to 9 | Includes bibliographical references and index.
Identifiers: ISBN: 9781678209506 (hardcover) | ISBN: 9781678209513 (eBook)
The complete Library of Congress record is available at www.loc.gov.

CONTENTS

AT A GLANCE	4
INTRODUCTION STOLEN ART	6
CHAPTER ONE ETHICAL PROBLEMS	12
CHAPTER TWO QUALITY OF LIFE	26
CHAPTER THREE HARM TO SOCIETY	38
CHAPTER FOUR PHYSICAL HARM	50
Glossary	58
Source Notes	59
For Further Research	60
Index	62
Image Credits	63
About the Author	64

AT A GLANCE

- Artificial intelligence (AI) is the ability of a computer to do tasks usually done by humans.

- AI systems can take in data, study its patterns, and output text, images, and other creative work.

- Many artists, authors, and others in creative fields are concerned about AI copying their work.

- AI has shown a tendency to create biased results when its training data contains biases.

- Experts worry that AI-generated content could be used to trick or confuse people.

- AI can lead to mistrust in people because it can be an unreliable source of information.

- Some experts argue that AI should be regulated in a way that holds its creators accountable when things go wrong.

- AI can affect people's jobs, how people view relationships, the quality of health care, and the environment.

- Some AI experts believe AI poses a risk of human extinction.

INTRODUCTION

STOLEN ART

Nick just won an art contest at school. He feels proud. When Nick gets home, he checks his Instagram feed. But what Nick sees makes his heart go cold. His art is on the screen. But it looks different from when he last saw it. It's not what he created. He thinks his classmates used artificial intelligence (AI) software to change his art. And they did it in a way that makes fun of him.

Discovering that a creative work has been altered using AI tools can be frustrating.

Nick gets an alert on his phone. It's from his AI personal assistant. It noticed the reactions to his art on social media.

Instagram is owned by Meta, the company that owns Facebook.

The assistant tells him that he is talented. It suggests he take a walk to calm down. Nick gets more upset. He does not want to calm down. He wants others to stop changing his art. His feelings of pride turn to anger. Nick needs to find out why they doing this. He wants them to stop.

Nick contacts the AI company that made the software his classmates used to change his art. He reports the revised art. But the AI company claims the art is original. Nick decides to follow the advice of his **chatbot**. He takes a walk. But when he gets home, Nick is still upset. His problem has not been solved.

The story of Nick and his artwork is fictional. But experts believe stories like Nick's may become more common in the future. There are many ways AI can be used to cause harm. Some of these tactics are being used already. Unfair use of someone's work is one of them.

WHAT IS ARTIFICIAL INTELLIGENCE?

AI is a computer's ability to do tasks usually done by humans. AI works by gathering **data**. It then looks for patterns. AI applies what it learns to new data. Often, AI is helpful. It can forecast weather. It helps doctors treat patients. AI can even drive cars. But AI can also hurt people and society. It can create ethical problems. These are problems related to what is right and wrong. AI might worsen people's quality of life. AI can take over

Artificial intelligence searches databases for patterns and connections between content. It then applies those patterns to new material.

people's jobs. It can affect relationships. And it may even cause physical harm to people and the world.

CHAPTER ONE

ETHICAL PROBLEMS

AI helps humans in many ways. Personal assistants can make life easier. Personal playlists are one way AI makes life more fun.

Yet AI can create ethical problems. It may copy the work of others. It can spread harmful **stereotypes**. It can be used to invade people's privacy. AI can even help governments control people.

Image generator apps have become popular ways to create content. These apps pull art from different online sources to create a work that matches what the user requests.

OpenAI's app ChatGPT has made it possible to write an entire song, book, or report with a few basic prompts.

COPIED WORK

AI can create stories, songs, news articles, and more. One example of this type of AI is ChatGPT. This is a chatbot created by the company OpenAI. The chatbot is trained on books, articles, and other texts. AI looks for patterns in language. It uses these patterns to guess what word should come next. This is how it creates text. A person can ask ChatGPT questions. The AI software gives answers. It uses the information it was trained on to write text.

People disagree about how AI software should be trained. Close to 200,000 books were used to train Meta's AI language model. OpenAI used books and articles to train ChatGPT, too. But the authors were not asked for permission to use their work. They were not paid, either.

Several authors have sued these companies. They say it was illegal for their work to be used without permission. They want to be credited and paid for their work. They also want to decide whether or not their work can be used to train AI. Some authors also worry that AI could be used to write books. AI systems use texts they are trained on in their responses. This includes authors' stories. Authors worry that text written by AI could replace books by human authors.

    Artists are having the same problem. Image generators are tools that use AI to create pictures. They are trained with art created by humans. AI makes art that copies these same styles. Three visual artists took a company called Stability AI to court. Their lawsuit states, "The harm to artists is not hypothetical—works generated by A.I. Image Products 'in the style' of a particular artist are already sold on the internet, [taking] commissions from the artists themselves."[1] Many creators believe AI harms their ability to make money from their work.

Several AI companies claim the works created are legal. They state that these

In the lawsuit, it was determined that Stability AI's use of artists' works to train AI was a copyright violation.

works fall under **fair use**. They say the original work inspired the new text or art. Some AI companies have said they will protect those who use their AI tools from legal action. These include Google, Microsoft, and Adobe. This means that if people are taken to court for using AI tools, these companies will take legal responsibility. But many companies have rules users must follow for this to apply.

STEREOTYPES

AI has already shown it can spread stereotypes. The technology is trained using images and text from the internet. But this content often contains biases. If the AI is trained using biased content, that's what it creates. These biases mean

While most Americans don't think AI should be used to make hiring decisions, 28 percent are in favor of using AI to sort through résumés.

many AI systems appear to favor white men. For example, Amazon used AI to review résumés. The company hoped this would save them time in the hiring process. But the AI tool preferred male applicants. This type of bias could make it difficult for women applying for jobs.

In another example, AI often showed images of Muslim men for the word *terrorist*. But in the United States, white men are responsible for three times more terrorist attacks than Muslim men. Biases like these concern experts. They worry biases in AI systems may negatively affect the lives of many people.

PRIVACY

AI gathers information. It uses this information to predict people's thoughts and actions. People are tracked by many of the devices they use every day. This includes phones, computers, and smart home devices. The amount of data AI collects will likely increase in the future. For example, AI can combine new data with data from the past. It can also compare data gathered from many devices.

Companies collect data about people to make money. Sometimes they use data to customize ads. They may also sell the

In some countries, AI monitoring systems are used to track people in public places. Systems like this were used during the COVID-19 pandemic to identify people who had the illness.

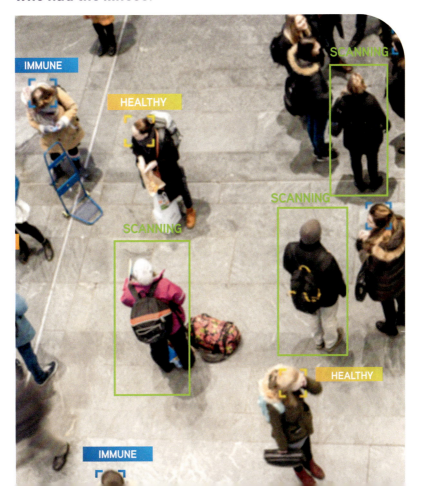

data to other companies. They use this data to try to sell people products.

The amount of data in the world doubles every two years. Many people are concerned about the use of their data. It is not always clear where this data is stored. It is also hard to know who has access to it. Some people worry their data will be used in a way they don't like.

AI in the News

In May of 2023, Amazon was fined $25 million. Companies are not supposed to store data from children. But the Federal Trade Commission said Amazon kept children's voice recordings from its digital assistant, Alexa. It used these to improve its algorithms. Amazon kept these recordings even after parents asked that they be deleted.

CONTROL

Sometimes, AI is used to control more than people's purchases. AI also uses people's data to control the content they see. This can prevent people from seeing social media posts from people with different opinions.

Governments can also use AI to watch their citizens. China is one example. It uses AI to track its citizens. This nation has more than 500 million cameras that follow people's activities. These cameras use **facial recognition**. They combine the information they gather with people's data online. This could include following shopping or social media activity.

Alfred Ng was a senior reporter for *POLITICO*. He states, "The threat of public

Going forward, facial recognition systems will likely become more common. They can be used to gain entry to businesses and electronic devices.

humiliation through facial recognition helps Chinese officials direct over a billion people toward what it considers acceptable behavior, from what you wear to how you cross the street."[2] This changes the way people act. More than eighty countries have bought **surveillance** systems from China. Experts believe this technology needs to be better **regulated**.

CHAPTER TWO

QUALITY OF LIFE

AI can have positive and negative effects on quality of life. This is how much people enjoy their lives. Quality of life is impacted by how safe, healthy, and comfortable people feel.

AI could cause people to lose trust in technology. People could become too dependent on technology. The lack of **accountability** among the companies that

Many people rely on AI technology, such as GPS mapping apps, every day. These technologies are convenient, but it also means people may lose the ability to navigate on their own.

create AI products is also an issue. This could also make life harder for people.

CREATING MISTRUST

AI can control what people see online. It also controls how often they see it. The content AI chooses to share can change

Social media companies use AI algorithms to fill people's feeds with advertisements that match the content they interact with.

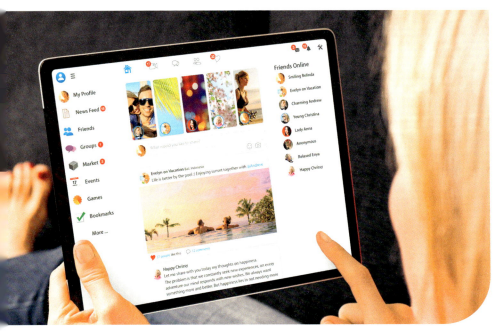

how people think. But the information AI shares cannot always be trusted. This is because AI sometimes shares false content.

Dr. Bobby Hoffman is a professor at the University of Central Florida. He is an expert in educational psychology. Hoffman says, "Purchasing options and consumer decisions can be manipulated by how AI presents and delivers responses."[3] This means the information AI provides could change the decisions people make. It can convince them to make choices or buy products they otherwise wouldn't. This is why many people do not trust AI with their data.

AI is trained to find patterns in data. Knowing these patterns helps AI provide answers. But AI can't always find answers.

Instead, it plugs in its best guess. Experts call this hallucinating. AI is trained to share answers that seem reasonable. It presents its answers as if they are facts. This makes it hard to know when AI gives an answer that is not true.

When people trust AI without question, it can lead to problems. For example, a doctor could trust an incorrect diagnosis given by AI. This could affect a person's health. Voters could trust false information AI shares on social media platforms. This could change how they vote. Developers are trying to solve these problems. But they worry that fixing them could affect how well AI does tasks.

Those who trust AI completely may be tricked by another form of false information.

ChatGPT answers questions based on the content it has access to online. Not all of the answers it gives are true.

A deepfake is when AI is used to make something that seems real but is not. For example, someone could use AI to create a video of a friend, celebrity, or politician. They could show this person saying or doing something they never said or did. This can fool people into believing something that is not true. Deepfakes can be used to

Computer scientists trained AI to play chess. IBM's Deep Blue supercomputer defeated chess champion Garry Kasparov in 1997.

convince people to support a cause or vote for a political candidate. They could lead people to create unrest within society.

OVERDEPENDENCE

There are also risks of people becoming too dependent on AI. The more people rely on

AI to do things for them, the less likely they are to think for themselves. But humans must learn when to trust AI and when to question it. Developers are trying to find ways to solve this issue. Having AI explain how it solves each problem is one idea. The AI could provide sources for its information. This can help people see how AI found the answers. It could help people see errors in AI's reasoning.

AI keeps improving. Computers can beat humans in checkers and chess. In 2011, AI beat humans in the game show *Jeopardy!* AI is not just outsmarting people at games. The bar exam is a test people take to become lawyers. The ChatGPT version 3.5 was released by OpenAI in November 2022. It scored in the bottom 10 percent on this test. But in March 2023, OpenAI released ChatGPT version 4.0. AI scored in the top 10 percent on the law exam.

Some believe that AI will eventually become smarter than all humans put together. If this happens, experts think people may lose the drive to learn and create new things. Author Bernard Marr studies technology. He makes predictions

AI in the Movies

WALL-E, *The Mitchells vs the Machines*, and *I, Robot* are movies. They show fictional accounts of how the future might look with AI. They explore how AI might react to different situations. In some movies, AI is caring and helpful to humans. In others, it wants to destroy them. The movies also show how humans might fight back.

about the future. He says, "Overreliance on AI systems may lead to a loss of creativity, critical thinking skills, and human intuition."[4] They say humans need this to keep a sense of what makes them human.

LACK OF ACCOUNTABILITY

Companies that create AI often don't share details about their work. This is because they do not want other companies to take their ideas and improve upon them. They also do not want people to use their ideas to cause harm. But keeping these secrets can harm users and society. For example, many developers do not share how their AI models were trained. They do not share what data was used to train them. Without this information, it is hard to regulate AI.

This makes it hard to know if AI is safe to use. It allows issues such as bias to affect the results.

AI can cause major problems. For example, **autonomous** cars driven by AI software have hit and killed people. But there are no regulations to determine who is at fault. When mistakes happen, people and companies often blame the computer or each other. No one is held accountable. Experts believe AI companies should explain how the technology works. The US government and AI experts are working together to regulate AI. But experts say they have a long way to go.

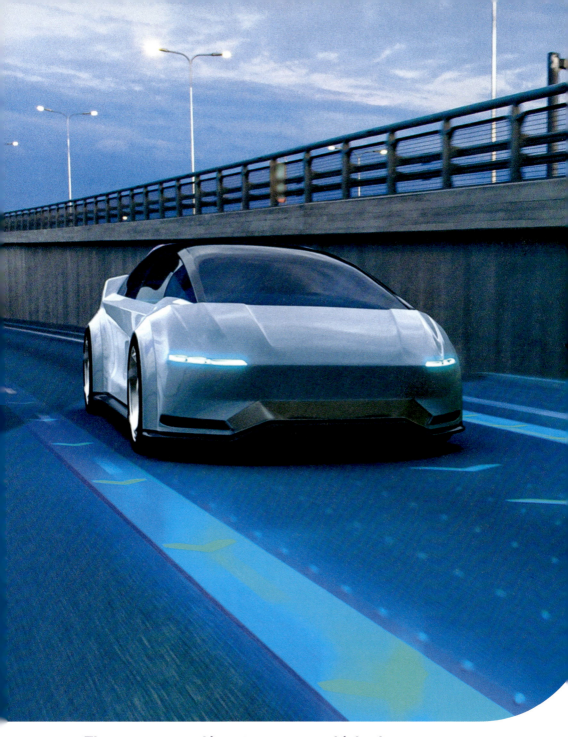

The sensors used in autonomous vehicles have sometimes failed, causing crashes that resulted in deaths.

CHAPTER THREE

HARM TO SOCIETY

Many people are concerned about the use of AI in daily life. Adults were asked about AI in 2023. In the survey, 52 percent felt more worried about AI than excited. Another 36 percent felt equally excited and concerned. And only 10 percent felt more excited than concerned.

Some people worry about how AI could be used at their jobs. Another concern

Some people are concerned that AI will take over more jobs in the future, including package delivery positions.

TOP CONCERNS ABOUT ARTIFICIAL INTELLIGENCE IN THE UNITED STATES

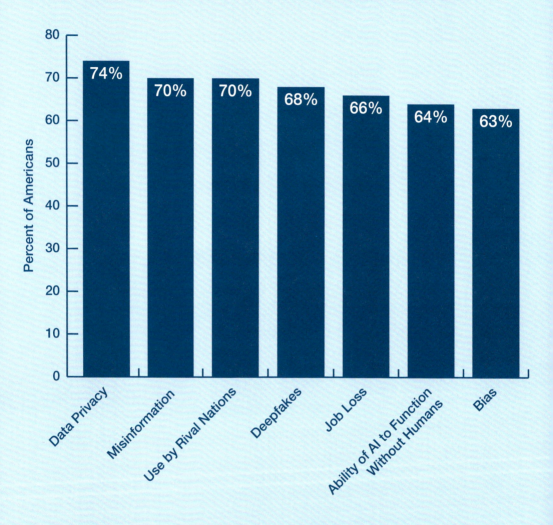

Source: Bergur Thormundsson, "Share of Adults in the United States Who Were Concerned About Issues Related to Artificial Intelligence (AI) as of February 2023," Statista, April 18, 2023. www.statista.com.

American adults have many concerns about how AI will affect their lives in the future. The graph above shows some of the issues they are most worried about.

is how AI might be used in health care. AI could also harm relationships and the environment.

JOBS

Experts believe AI will change nearly every job. Some jobs will be affected more than others. These include customer service and repetitive jobs such as data entry.

Many experts think AI will help workers be more productive. But AI caused the loss of nearly 4,000 jobs in May 2023 alone. AI will continue to take over jobs. This could leave more people unemployed.

There is also concern that AI will lead to a larger gap between the rich and poor. Daron Acemoglu and Simon Johnson are professors at the Massachusetts Institute of Technology. They state, "Technologies develop according to the vision and choices of those in positions of power. . . . when these choices are left entirely in the hands of a small elite, you should expect that group to receive most of the benefits, while everyone else bears the costs—potentially for a long time."[5] Wealthy people are often the ones making decisions about new technologies. Their choices tend to help them. This can make life harder for people in lower-paying jobs.

RELATIONSHIPS

People might think human relationships won't be affected by AI. But that's not true. AI has made it possible for a person to have virtual voices that always agree with them.

AI-generated worlds make it possible for people to interact with new people.

AI chatbots are made to listen, agree, and support people in the way that they want. Over time, this might make people choose chatbots over friends. Friends are more likely to disagree or share an honest opinion. Anne T. Griffin is an AI ethics expert. "On the emotional side," she says, "we could see individuals struggle to develop true emotional maturity in

43

Medical studies have often focused on white males.

human-to-human relationships."[6] It may be easier to talk to chatbots. But people find more joy when talking with humans. The more time humans spend with AI, the less happy they might become.

HEALTH CARE

AI could help doctors provide better health care. It helps read medical scans. AI can study patient data. It can also help develop vaccines. But there are some ways AI negatively affects health care. Health care is very personal. What works for one person might not work for others. Much of health care is based research done on white men. This means a lot of the information AI studies is based on this group. This adds to biases in health care. These biases negatively impact women and people of color.

Using people's private health data to train AI is also a risk. It is important that companies request permission from patients before using their health data. Some people may be willing to share their health information to train AI. Others may not want their personal data being fed into an AI algorithm.

THE ENVIRONMENT

AI can harm the environment. For example, training AI takes a lot of electricity. It can emit hundreds of thousands of pounds of carbon dioxide. AI sifts through large amounts of data. This data is stored in the cloud. AI uses processors that are stored in huge data warehouses. These create a lot of heat. Energy is used to cool the data centers. This adds to AI's carbon footprint.

AI also requires lots of computer hardware. This hardware is made of minerals such as copper, tin, silver, and zinc. These minerals are found deep underground. Mining is needed to get to these materials. This can harm the Earth.

Powering AI

By the year 2027, the amount of power used by AI is expected to match that of a small country. AI will use as much energy as countries such as the Netherlands and Sweden. Experts believe that more than 6 percent of the world's energy will be used to run AI by the year 2030.

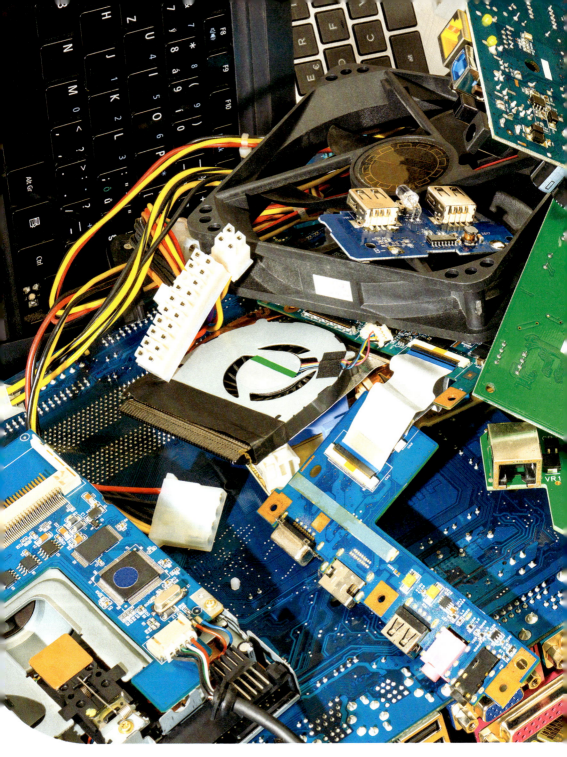

E-waste can include computer circuit boards, hard drives, or devices such as outdated phones.

AI also creates a lot of e-waste. This is electronic waste such as old devices and their parts. All hardware used for AI will someday need to be thrown away. About 85 percent of e-waste is burned or thrown in landfills. Toxic elements are inside 70 percent of this waste. This is bad for people and the planet.

CHAPTER FOUR

PHYSICAL HARM

Experts think there is a risk that AI could cause physical harm. In 2023, 36 percent of AI experts worried the technology could lead to issues as serious as a nuclear disaster. AI could be used in wars. It could be told to harm people. Or AI might act on its own to harm people.

Some are concerned AI could lead to human extinction. Most experts believe the

Some people fear that developments in AI technology may lead to physical harm of humans. The military's use of AI is one source of these concerns.

chances of this are very low. But it is a risk that some people are taking seriously.

WAR

AI is being developed for use in war. Militaries around the world are studying ways AI could be used. In 2014, the United States began looking into autonomous technology for use in war.

Unmanned ships are used by militaries around the world to monitor the movements of other nations' fleets.

Many countries already have autonomous ships. These have cameras and radar but no people onboard. They can keep watch over certain areas.

Some of these ships can use weapons. But many do not yet include them. Amir Alon is the senior director of an Israeli defense firm that created such ships. "It can engage autonomously, but we don't recommend it," Alon said. "We don't want to start World War III."[7] AI-powered drones have also been developed. These can move on their own. They can even coordinate their movements in a group. Other AI-operated machines are being developed. These include battle tanks.

The use of autonomous ships and drones poses ethical issues. People are concerned about leaving the decision of who dies in battle to technology. Someone needs to be held responsible if anything goes wrong. Some experts think international treaties will be needed. This could help countries around the world agree on how AI might be used in war.

EXTINCTION

There is something even more concerning than the use of AI in war. Many AI experts, scientists, and world leaders are worried that AI could wipe humans off the planet entirely. There are many ways this could happen.

AI could be used by terrorists or governments to cause harm. It could help create weapons of mass destruction.

Cyberattacks launched by AI-powered systems could be a real threat in the future.

Cyberattacks could spiral out of control. This could lead to a breakdown of society.

Another concern is that AI could try to end the human race. AI could eventually learn to train itself. Most AI software has intelligence in one or two areas. Someday, AI could gain general intelligence. This means it would have access to data in many different areas. It would have the brainpower of a human. AI could have

As AI continues to improve, experts are working on plans to monitor and maintain control of AI-powered systems to keep humans safe.

the collective intelligence of all humans someday. As a result, AI could outsmart humans. This would mean it could stop all attempts to shut it down. Robots powered by AI could create more robots. These scenarios may sound like they are out of a science fiction book or movie. But experts are taking these concerns seriously.

AI experts are thinking about ways to protect the public. This is hard because AI is being developed very quickly. Countries from around the world are meeting to plan how to prevent AI dangers. Some think AI could be smarter than humans by the early 2030s.

Open Letter from Experts

AI experts signed a letter to the public in May 2023. The letter said, "Mitigating the risk of extinction from AI should be a global priority alongside other . . . risks such as pandemics and nuclear war." The letter called for companies to pause work on more advanced AI. But many experts kept developing more advanced AI.

Oliver Darcy, "Experts are Warning AI Could Lead to Human Extinction. Are We Taking It Seriously Enough?," CNN, May 31, 2023. www.cnn.com.

GLOSSARY

accountability

taking responsibility for one's actions

autonomous

able to control itself

chatbot

computer software designed to communicate with humans

data

factual information

facial recognition

technology that can recognize or identify a person's face

fair use

legal concept that states parts of copyrighted works can be used without permission from the copyright owner

regulated

controlled with rules

stereotypes

opinions or beliefs about a group of people

surveillance

keeping watch over someone or something

SOURCE NOTES

CHAPTER ONE: ETHICAL PROBLEMS

1. Quoted in Ella Feldman, "Are A.I. Image Generators Violating Copyright Laws?" *Smithsonian*, January 24, 2023. www.smithsonianmag.com.

2. Alfred Ng, "How China Uses Facial Recognition to Control Human Behavior." *CNET*, August 11, 2020. www.cnet.com.

CHAPTER TWO: QUALITY OF LIFE

3. Bobby Hoffman, "The Hidden Mental Manipulation of Generative AI," *Psychology Today*, August 3, 2023. www.psychologytoday.com.

4. Bernard Marr, "The 15 Biggest Risks of Artificial Intelligence," *Forbes*, June 2, 2023. www.forbes.com.

CHAPTER THREE: HARM TO SOCIETY

5. Daron Acemoglu and Simon Johnson, "Choosing AI's Impact on the Future of Work," *Stanford Social Innovation Review*, October 25, 2023. www.ssir.org.

6. Quoted in Miles Klee, "'Cyber-heartbreak' and Privacy Risks: The Perils of Dating an AI," *Rolling Stone*, May 17, 2023. www.rollingstone.com.

CHAPTER FOUR: PHYSICAL HARM

7. Quoted in Will Knight, "The AI-Powered, Totally Autonomous Future of War is Here," *Wired*, July 25, 2023. www.wired.com.

FOR FURTHER RESEARCH

BOOKS

Jennifer Kaul, *The Potential of Artificial Intelligence*. San Diego, CA: BrightPoint Press, 2025.

George Anthony Kulz, *Artificial Intelligence and the Changing Job Market*. San Diego, CA: BrightPoint Press, 2025.

Dr. Claire Quigley, *Simply Artificial Intelligence*. New York: DK, 2023.

INTERNET SOURCES

Renée Cho, "AI's Growing Carbon Footprint," *Columbia Climate School*, June 9, 2023. www.news.climate.columbia.edu.

Devin Coldewey, "Age of AI: Everything You Need to Know About Artificial Intelligence," *Tech Crunch*, August 4, 2023. www.techcrunch.com.

Aruna Pattam, "Artificial Intelligence, Defined in Simple Terms," *HCL Tech*, September 16, 2021. hcltech.com.

WEBSITES

OpenAI
www.openai.com

OpenAI is the company that developed ChatGPT. Its website explains the uses for OpenAI products and provides information about types of AI. The site also includes articles about OpenAI research.

Teens in AI
www.teensinai.com

Teens in AI is a company that helps teenagers learn about technology and related career possibilities.

Why AI
www.ai.google

Why AI is a website run by Google that discusses making AI accessible to everyone. It includes articles about how AI is being used responsibly to help people and society.

INDEX

accountability, 26, 35–36, 54
Acemoglu, Daron, 41–42
Alon, Amir, 53
Amazon, 19, 22
autonomous vehicles, 36, 52–53

biases, 18–20, 36, 40, 45–46

carbon footprint, 46–47
chatbots, 9, 14–15, 43–45
ChatGPT, 14–15, 33–34
control, 12, 23–25, 28
copied works, 12, 14–18
cyberattacks, 55

data use, 10, 20–23, 29, 36, 46
deepfakes, 30–32, 40

e-waste, 49
environment, 41, 46–49
ethical problems, 10, 12–25, 53–54

facial recognition, 23–25
fair use, 17–18

general intelligence, 55–56
Google, 18
Griffin, Anne T., 43–44

health care, 41, 45–46
Hoffman, Bobby, 29
human extinction, 50–52, 54–57

image generators, 17

job loss, 40, 41–42
Johnson, Simon, 41–42

Marr, Bernard, 35
mistakes, 33, 36
mistrust, 28–32

Ng, Alfred, 25
nuclear disaster, 50, 57

OpenAI, 14–15, 33–34
overdependence, 32–35

physical harm, 11, 50–57
privacy, 12, 20–23, 40

quality of life, 11, 26–36

relationships, 11, 41, 42–45
robots, 56

Stability AI, 17
stereotypes, 12, 18–20
surveillance, 23, 25

tracking, 20, 23

wars, 50, 52–54

IMAGE CREDITS

Cover: © Andrey_Popov/Shutterstock Images
5: © aslysun/Shutterstock Images
7: © Monkey Business Images/Shutterstock Images
8: © Wichayada Suwanachun/Shutterstock Images
11: © NicoElNino/Shutterstock Images
13: © Nuva Frames/Shutterstock Images
14: © Arsenii Palivoda/Shutterstock Images
16: © Gorodenkoff/Shutterstock Images
19: © MMD Creative/Shutterstock Images
21: © Tint Media/Shutterstock Images
24: © Zapp2Photo/Shutterstock Images
27: © Monopoly919/Shutterstock Images
28: © Kaspars Grinvalds/Shutterstock Images
31: © Thapana_Studio/Shutterstock Images
32: © Gorodenkoff/iStockphoto
37: © Gorodenkoff/Shutterstock Images
39: © David Olivera/Shutterstock Images
40: © Red Line Editorial
43: © Gorodenkoff/Shutterstock Images
44: © a24/Shutterstock Images
48: © KPixMining/Shutterstock Images
51: © TSViPhoto/Shutterstock Images
52: © Billy Watkins/Shutterstock Images
55: © Teerachai Jampanak/Shutterstock Images
56: © Gorodenkoff/Shutterstock Images

ABOUT THE AUTHOR

Jennifer Kaul is an author of young adult literature, a former educator, and a cautious optimist. Many of Kaul's pieces stem from the happenings in our world and the what-ifs that swirl around her head as a result. Through her writing, she hopes to encourage thought, spark conversation, and make the world a better place.